THE ADVENTURES OF TOM SAWYER

THE ADVENTURES OF TOM SAWYER

Mark Twain

An imprint of Om Books International

First published in 2013

An imprint of Om Books International

Corporate & Editorial Office
A-12, Sector 64, Noida 201 301
Uttar Pradesh, India
Phone: +91 120 477 4100
Email: editorial@ombooks.com
Website: www.ombooksinternational.com

Sales Office
4379/4B, Prakash House, Ansari Road
Darya Ganj, New Delhi 110 002, India
Phone: +91 11 2326 3363, 2326 5303
Fax: +91 11 2327 8091
Email: sales@ombooks.com
Website: www.ombooks.com

Adapted by Subhojit Sanyal
Illustrations: Dipankar Mukharjee, Manoj Kumar Prasad, Anshuman Pandey

ISBN: 978-93-83202-50-8

Printed in India

10 9 8 7 6 5 4 3 2 1

Contents

1. The Great Whitewash — 7
2. Tom Meets Becky — 15
3. Heartbreak For Tom — 23
4. Tragedy In The Graveyard — 29
5. Tom And His Guilty Conscience — 43
6. The Cat And The Pain-killer — 51
7. The Pirates Set Sail — 61
8. Tom Visits Home — 79
9. The Pirates Return — 87
10. Back Home Again — 101
11. Aunt Polly Learns The Truth — 119
12. The Salvation Of Muff Potter — 131
13. Digging For The Buried Treasure — 141
14. Trembling On The Trail — 155
15. Huck Saves The Widow — 167
16. Lost In The Cave — 179
17. Escape! — 191
18. Buried Treasure — 203
19. A Home For Huck — 225
20. Respectable Huck Joins The Gang — 231
About The Author — 236
Characters — 236
Questions — 237

Chapter One

The Great Whitewash

Tom Sawyer was a troublesome boy who loved adventure. As an orphan, he lived with his Aunt Polly, cousin Mary and half-brother Sid. He was very mischievous, and Sid often complained about him to Aunt Polly. He would hide when called to do errands for his aunt, steal sweets and other goodies and be generally mischievous. Aunt Polly, however, could never bring herself to hit the naughty boy because he was her dead sister's son and she loved him dearly.

One day, she found out from Sid that Tom skipped school to go swimming. On top of that,

he had a fight with another boy and came home covered in dust, his clothes tattered.

Aunt Polly was furious!

As a punishment, he was told to whitewash thirty yards of fence on a sunny Sunday afternoon. This was very troublesome for such a mischievous boy who would have preferred to play ball or swim on such a day. And so, Tom stood with a brush and paint all alone by the fence.

The fence seemed huge to him and it would take all day to give it just one coat of paint. He was further saddened at the thought of all the fun he would miss out on because of this task, and how his friends would laugh at him.

He had toys, marbles and trash in his pockets and thought he might be able to bribe someone to do it for him. But he would still not have an entire day of fun. Then an idea struck him! He began to slowly painting the fence. After some time, Ben Rogers came strolling eating a big, juicy apple that made Tom's mouth water. But he pretended to ignore Ben as he painted the fence.

Ben was on his way to the river to swim and exclaimed, "What a pity that you have to work and can't come swimming, Tom!"

Tom looked at Ben and said that this was not work because he enjoyed painting the fence.

Ben was surprised and said that one could not possibly enjoy such a task, to which Tom replied, "It isn't every day that a boy gets a chance to paint a fence."

Tom's enjoyment made Ben curious and jealous and he too wanted to give it a try. However, Tom said that Aunt Polly would be angry and refused to give the brush to Ben. He bragged that she trusted him to do this important job by himself.

Ben continued to plead, asking Tom to allow him to paint just a little bit of the fence but Tom kept refusing. Finally, Ben offered Tom his apple in exchange for the privilege of whitewashing the fence, which was exactly the opportunity Tom was looking for.

Sitting in the shade of a tree, Tom munched the apple while Ben sweated in the hot sun, doing Tom's task. Seeing that it was so easy to fool Ben, Tom struck similar deals with the other neighbourhood boys as they passed the fence.

By mid-afternoon, the fence was completely whitewashed and Tom, with his pockets full of toys and other treasures of the boys, realized that he could make others do his tasks for him by making them seem fun to do.

He went inside and told his Aunt Polly that the fence was completely whitewashed and that he wanted to go play now. She, obviously, thought he was lying but when she went to check, she was surprised to see that it was indeed completely done.

She was very pleased and rewarded him for his dexterity by offering him a big, juicy apple and permitted him to go out, but told him to be back by dinnertime.

Tom agreed with a smile, stole a sugared doughnut when she wasn't looking and went out.

As Tom was roaming in the street, he saw a blonde girl in Jeff Thatcher's garden. She was so pretty that he instantly fell in love with her!

He stood on his hands and tried other silly tricks to attract her attention and impress her but, unfortunately for him, he was ignored by her. Realising his failure, Tom swore that within the week he would win her love.

With a full heart and satisfied stomach, he skipped down the road, dreaming of romance and adventure.

Chapter Two

Tom Meets Becky

The next morning, like every Monday morning, Tom was miserable as he had to go to school. He began to plan ways of skipping school. He was a healthy boy and could not find anything wrong with himself to give the excuse that he was sick, and so, would not be able attend school.

After some deep thinking, he realized that one of his upper front teeth was loose. He immediately felt lucky. But just as he was about to pretend to moan and groan in pain, he remembered that Aunt Polly was adept at wrenching out loose teeth and forgot all about the scheme as he did not want to feel that horrible pain.

He kept thinking and suddenly remembered a doctor describing his patient's illness that made him unable to leave his bed for a fort night and almost lose his finger.

Tom had a sore toe that he had neither noticed nor thought about in days but, without knowing the details of that patient, he wondered if he could fool Aunt Polly. So, he began moaning and wailing.

Sid, who slept in the next bed, did not even hear his groans and kept sleeping soundly. Tom increased the volume of his moans until finally Sid woke up and ran downstairs to inform Aunt Polly of Tom's agony.

"I think he's dying!" gasped a terrified Sid to Aunt Polly.

"Rubbish!" she replied but hurried upstairs to see what the matter was. She became pale when she saw Tom's condition.

"Aunt Polly, it's my sore toe. I think it's about to fall off!" wailed Tom.

At this, Aunt Polly heaved a sigh of relief and sat down laughing and crying a bit. She told him to stop the nonsense and get dressed for school immediately.

At this, Tom moaned loudly, "Oh, but Aunt, it hurts so much that I forgot about my loose tooth."

As soon as he said those words, he was in trouble. She examined his tooth, tied a silk thread to it and began the process of extracting it. Tom cried and begged her to stop but she was not to be dissuaded. She brought a hot log from the kitchen, thrust it dangerously close to his face and when Tom jumped back in fright, he saw the tooth dangling on the silk thread.

The gap between Tom's teeth made him the object of attention and envy in the eyes of the other boys, on the way to school. Seeing this, he felt that maybe the pain was worth it.

When he almost reached school, he met the son of the town drunkard, Huckleberry Finn. Huck wore rags and hand-me-down clothes and was not bound by any rule. He slept in doorways and empty barns and the envied by every boy in town because he neither had to go to church, nor school. He was, however, treated as an outcast by the boys' mothers.

Tom waved at Huck and got engaged in a serious conversation concerning the curing of warts. He also exchanged his extracted tooth for a tick that Huck showed him.

The negotiations for exchange made him late for class.

When Mr. Dobins demanded an explanation, he was about to create an elaborate lie when he noticed the pretty blonde girl sitting in his classroom. He also noticed that the only empty chair left in the classroom was next to her.

So Tom replied, "I was with Huckleberry Finn."

Everyone, including the teacher, was shocked. Nobody openly admitted to being in the company of the town's outcast. The teacher whipped him with a stick and, as punishment, made him sit with the girls. This was exactly what Tom had wanted. He was in pain but felt it was a small price to pay to sit beside the girl he was in love with.

The girl, however, ignored him and shook her head even when he offered her a peach.

So, he began drawing on his slate, covering it with his arm so that she would not be able to see. He seemed to concentrate deeply on his work.

Soon the girl became curious and wanted to see his sketch. Tom pretended to ignore her. She finally whispered, "Let me see."

Tom showed her part of the drawing which was a house with a brick chimney set in the background of a blue sky.

She was impressed, told him to add people and claimed that she could not draw. Tom whispered, "It's easy, I'll show you."

The girl's name was Becky Thatcher and she agreed to spend lunch recess with Tom and learn how to draw from him.

Tom returned to his drawing and this time refused to show her his slate. Becky pleaded for a while and he finally showed her the part he had covered. He had written boldly, "I love you." Becky blushed but was pleased.

Chapter Three

Heartbreak For Tom

It was a boring day and Tom soon began playing with the tick he got from Huck. Tom and his best friend, Joe Harper, began poking it with a pin to make it change it direction of crawling. They drew a territory on Joe's slate with chalk and were so engrossed in their game that they did not realize that the class grew quiet and Mr. Dobins was watching over their heads.

They were whipped with his stick as punishment.

At lunch, Becky watched Tom draw and was very impressed.

Tom then got her engaged to him by making her promise to never love anyone else but him. He told her to seal the promise with a kiss. She first hesitated but then allowed him to kiss her, as he told her that they would always walk to school together and choose each other at parties.

"We'll always be with each other when nobody is looking," said Tom.

Becky thought it was lovely being engaged but Tom spoiled it by foolishly saying, "It's fun! Why me and Amy Lawrence…"

He stopped abruptly but the damage was done. Becky began crying and refused to believe him when he said that he no longer cared for Amy.

Tom began walking up and down the yard but then returned to Becky who would not stop crying, telling her that she was his only love.

Tom finally took out his most important treasure, a brass doorknob, from his pocket and offered it to her but she threw it on the ground, quite heartbroken.

Enraged and frustrated, Tom stomped out of school and did not return that afternoon.

Becky then regretted her actions and called out and looked for him but could not find him. She assumed that she lost him.

Chapter Four

Tragedy In The Graveyard

Having left Becky in a huff, Tom kept running through back roads until he was far away from school. He then sat by the side of a road, burying his chin on his palms and digging his elbows onto his knees. Life seemed to him nothing but pain and trouble. Becky Thatcher had treated him like a dog when he tried to tell her that he loved her.

"She'll be sorry someday," he swore to himself, "but then it'll be too late!"

Tom began thinking of death. He saw a future in his mind where his poor body would be carried into a church, and Becky and Aunt Polly would cry their eyes out. They would then say good

things about him, about how he was a brave and wonderful boy but their words would not bring him back.

Tom's was suddenly awakened from his sorrowful musings by the presence of Huckleberry Finn. He immediately forgot all about his misery and began spiritedly playing the game, Robin Hood, with Huck.

They kept playing until Tom realized that it was almost dinnertime and said good bye to Huck, making plans to sneak out in the middle of the night and meet at the local graveyard where they would make plans and have adventures.

That night, Tom and Sid went to bed as usual at half past nine. Sid fell asleep but Tom with his mind full of hopes of new adventures kept waiting for Huck's signal to come down and meet him. He waited for a very long time and then finally heard Huck calling out, "Meow," which meant that he was waiting for Tom in the shed.

On hearing his call, Tom opened a window, and carefully climbed down to meet his friend.

Huck was holding a dead cat in his hands as their plan had been to swing it over a grave and see if this action could cure warts.

The boys walked all the way to an old graveyard on a hill which was about a mile and a half away from the village. It was an unkempt graveyard with grass and weed wildly growing everywhere. Lacking proper care, some of the older graves were so sunken that their gravestones could not even be seen.

Tom was a little frightened and whispered to Huck, "Do you think the dead people will like us being here?"

"I wish I knew," replied Huck. He too did not like the silent, solemn air of the graveyard.

And that was when Tom thought he heard something and held on to Huck's arm. The boys froze in fear.

"Did you hear it?" asked Tom, terrified. He thought he could hear something coming towards them.

Then they both saw a couple of silhouettes walking through the graveyard and directly towards them. One of the figures was swinging a lantern.

Huck trembled and whispered that those were surely devils. The figures were now close enough to see that there were three of them. Surely, Huck and Tom were in terrible danger.

"Can you pray?" asked Huck to Tom.

But just as Tom was about to begin praying, he recognized one of the figures as Muff Potter. He knew Muff's voice. And now the boys realized that all three were human.

As they sat silently, watching the three figures, their lantern revealed their faces to the boys who at once recognized the other two as young Dr. Robinson and fearsome Injun Joe, a murderer.

They had a wheelbarrow and Muff and Injun Joe were taking ropes and shovels from it as Dr. Robinson stood beside them, telling them to hurry up and dig up a grave before the moon came out.

They began digging and after some time, their shovels struck something wooden a coffin. They lifted the coffin, removed its lid and a took out the body. They placed the body in the wheelbarrow, covering it with a blanket.

Injun Joe said, "Now it's done. Give me five dollars more or I won't take it further."

The doctor exclaimed that he had paid advance to both.

Injun Joe, however, held a grudge against the doctor because he had been sentenced by the doctor's father to imprisonment for threatening his life and now, seeing his opportunity for revenge, raised his fist to the doctor's face.

Dr. Robinson was quick in avoiding Injun Joe's fist, and knocking him to the ground.

Then Muff began fighting the doctor and while the two were lashing out blows at each other, Injun Joe got on his feet. With hatred burning in his eyes, he picked up Muff's knife and turned towards the two fighters, waiting for a chance to strike the doctor.

Dr. Robinson managed to free himself from Muff's tight grasp and, seeing an opportunity, struck him on the head with a heavy gravestone. Muff fell down unconscious. At that very moment, Injun Joe used the knife to stab the doctor in his chest. The doctor fell on top of Muff, bleeding heavily.

Injun Joe stood looking at his two victims until the doctor groaned, gasped and was finally still. He then checked the doctor's pockets and took his money and other valuables. After that, Injun Joe placed the knife in Muff's open right palm.

By then, Muff had regained consciousness. He saw the knife in his hand, shuddered and dropped it aghast.

"How did this happen?" he asked Injun Joe, horrified at what he thought he had done.

Injun Joe told Muff that being highly drunk, Muff had got into a fight with Dr. Robinson and stabbed and killed him.

Though Muff first refused to believe Injun Joe's account of the incident, Joe said it with so much conviction, that Muff finally believed him. He then begged Injun Joe to keep it a secret.

This is exactly what Injun Joe was waiting for and, promising to not tell a word of Muff's crime to anyone, he left the graveyard with his partner.

The dead doctor, the blanketed corpse on the wheelbarrow and the coffin without its lid were left as they were.

The two boys, Huck and Tom, ran towards their village. On their way, they were frightened of every shadow and unable to speak because of the horrific actions they had just witnessed.

"What do you think will happen now, Huck?" asked Tom breathlessly as they entered the village.

Huck, gasping for air, replied, "There will surely be a hanging if Dr. Robinson is dead!"

The boys realized that they were the sole witnesses of the murder but were afraid that if they dared to point out who the real killer was, Injun Joe would not leave them alone and probably kill them too. Muff Potter had been unconscious during the entire stabbing episode so he could not be relied on to give witness against Injun Joe.

The boys went to a dilapidated, old building in the village to discuss about what to do next.

Huck told Tom that they would have to keep quiet about the whole matter and not breathe a word of it to anyone because if Injun Joe came to know that the two of them had witnessed his crime, he would not hesitate to kill them too.

Huck said they had to be sworn into secrecy. So the two boys scribbled on a piece of wood: HUCK FINN AND TOM SAWYER SWEAR THAT THEY WILL KEEP MUM AND WISH THAT THEY MAY DROP DOWN DEAD AND ROT IF THEY EVER TELL

They then pricked their fingers with a needle and marked their initials on the bark in blood.

They buried the bark underground, whispering magical incantations that they made up randomly from words that they had heard elsewhere. It was an important ceremony to them.

Having sealed their oath in blood, both Huck and Tom knew that neither would speak of that dreadful incident ever again.

They were about to part ways for the night when they were troubled by the baying of a dog. They thought it was a stray and were very scared because in their village there was a superstition that if a stray dog turned towards someone or their house and bayed, the person would die. Huck and Tom looked at each other, speechless in their fright. They stood absolutely still, without making any sound. After some time, thankfully, the dog turned away and left, still baying loudly. The boys decided that it was not them, and quickly left the abandoned building. Tom walked towards his home, still trembling at what he had seen in the graveyard and thinking about his oath.

Chapter Five

Tom And His Guilty Conscience

After saying goodbye to Huck, Tom climbed silently back through the window into his room. Undressing and creeping into his bed quietly, he was relieved that no one had come to know about his adventure. However, he did not know that Sid was only pretending to be asleep and was, in fact, awake and aware that Tom had gone out at night.

The next morning, when Tom woke up and realized that Sid was not in his bed and that no one had come to wake him up, he felt that something must be wrong. Feeling sleepy and sore, he quickly got dressed and went downstairs.

Aunt Polly was waiting for him and, after breakfast, took him aside, weeping, and said that she knew he had slipped out of the window last night. She told him that she had broken his heart by being so mischievous.

"It's no use, trying to raise you to be a good boy, Tom," the poor old woman wailed.

Tom felt miserable about hurting her and promised to mend his ways. He begged her for forgiveness and went to school feeling upset and depressed. He was so sad that he even forgot to get even with Sid for reporting to Aunt Polly about him.

Without making any sound, he slipped into his seat in class and found a hard, cold object wrapped in paper. When he removed the covering, he became even more saddened to see that it was the brass doorknob that he had given Becky. She had returned his gift, and it shocked him greatly.

But Tom did not have time to sit and be mournful. By noon, the entire village was in an uproar about Dr. Robinson's murder. Everybody seemed to be going towards the graveyard which was the scene of the murder. Forgetting entirely about his heartbreak, Tom joined the others.

The moment he reached the scene of the crime, he felt someone pinching his arm. It was Huck. The two boys looked at each other, feeling guilty about what they had witnessed and also fearful lest they be discovered.

Within a very short time, Injun Joe and Muff appeared too. There, in everyone's presence, Injun Joe told the sheriff about how the horrific crime had happened because Muff had drunkenly stabbed the doctor.

The knife that Injun Joe had used to kill the doctor belonged to Muff and it was as the crime weapon identified.

Huck and Tom stood aghast at the bare-faced lie. They knew that they were the only ones who could save an innocent man from being hanged but were too frightened to say anything. They were also bound by their oath.

On his part, Muff said that though he had wanted to run away, he was not able to. He had to come back to the scene of his crime as though pulled by some invisible force.

Muff was arrested. Tom and Huck felt that Injun Joe had sold himself to the devil and stared at him with curiosity and fear.

From then on, Tom's conscience kept disturbing him and he had trouble sleeping. Every night he would toss and turn and feel agitated but could do nothing about it.

But when Sid complained to Aunt Polly about Tom's behaviour and she questioned him, all he could mutter was, "It's nothing." But his hands shook and he spilled some of his coffee.

Sid, however, was very concerned and told Tom that he had begun talking in his sleep. "Last night you were saying something about blood and not telling someone something," said Sid suspiciously.

This made Aunt Polly think that perhaps Tom was having nightmares about the murder

because he had seen the body. Several others in the village were also having similar nightmares. Tom merely nodded his head in affirmation, but clever Sid thought that Tom was hiding something that he knew about the murder.

During this time, Tom would regularly visit the little prison and give small gifts to Muff through the jail window. These gifts included cigars and bits of fruits and food. Muff believed that it was Tom's way of thanking him for the times that they had gone fishing together. Tom, on the other hand, was giving him these gifts to try and calm his own guilty conscience.

Chapter Six

The Cat And The Pain-killer

Tom Sawyer was having a horrible time. Not only did he suffer from sleepless night, he was also saddened because Becky Thatcher had stopped coming to school. Tom began to stroll past her house, lounge around the street of her house and try to catch a glimpse of her face through a window. But it was all in vain. He was told that she had fallen ill and he became worried that she might die of her illness.

Every joy had left poor Tom's life. He kept away his bat, ball and other playthings, and seemed to lose interest in everything. It was difficult for him to bear each day as it passed.

His condition alarmed Aunt Polly. Tom was always a boy of high spirits and she had never seen him looking so low and lost. She tried all sorts of home-made remedies to cure him from his listlessness but nothing seemed to have any effect on him. Rather than getting better, Tom began to grow pale, morose and hardly showed any interest in day-to-day activities. Also, normally Tom would make a lot of fuss whenever Aunt Polly made him swallow medicines or take hot oatmeal baths but this new, sad, indifferent Tom didn't to care. His behaviour was shocking to Aunt Polly who was used to the naughty, playful, cheerful boy.

It was then that Aunt Polly saw a Pain-Killer medicine advertised in a magazine. Believing that it could help revive poor Tom, she immediately ordered some. She first tried it herself. It tasted awful. She thought that if Tom made a fuss about taking this disgusting tasting medicine, then he would at least be showing some of old spark.

She gave him a spoonful of it. At once, she saw a change coming over Tom. He seemed to take particular interest in the medicine.

In reality, Tom had become bored with his unhappy state of mind. He had also had enough of Aunt Polly's attempts to nurse him back to cheerfulness. It seemed to him that if he pretended to actually like the awful tasting medicine, he would have some fun. So he began asking for it all the time.

Finally, his constant request for the medicine began to annoy Aunt Polly and she told him to have it himself. What she had never expected was that Tom did not consume the medicine but poured it into a crack on the floor in the parlour.

One day, as Tom was throwing away a spoonful of the medicine in the same manner, his aunt's yellow cat, Peter, came into the parlour.

Peter looked intensely at the spoon in Tom's hand and seemed to be begging him for a taste.

"Don't ask for it unless you really want it, Peter," said Tom.

Peter meowed, indicating that he did indeed want to taste the medicine.

Tom warned him again, telling him to be absolutely certain that he wanted it.

Again Peter meowed, as though affirming his request.

Tom then held the cat, forcefully opened his mouth and poured the Pain Killer down his throat. Peter jumped into the air with a loud screech almost as if it was going to war. He rose on his hind feet and danced around. He then began running around the room, crashing against furniture, turning flower-pots over, tumbling everything in the vicinity and making an absolute mess of the room.

Aunt Polly rushed in the room, on hearing poor Peter's screeches and stood still in amazement as she saw the cat somersaulting in the air and flying out of the open window, carrying a few flowerpots with him.

Tom was lying on the floor, laughing so hard that tears streamed down his face. Gasping for

breath, he somehow managed to tell Aunt Polly what made the cat act so strangely. His old aunt admitted that it was a very cruel thing that Tom had done, but she also smiled at the same time because it showed that Tom was finally regaining his lost spirit.

Chapter Seven

The Pirates Set Sail

The next morning Tom reached school ahead of time. In fact, for the next few days, he made it a point to reach school ahead of time. He also grew a new habit of standing close to the gate of the schoolyard instead of playing with his classmates, as he earlier used to do.

Tom claimed to be sick and his countenance proved it. He seemed to be looking in all directions and finally, when he saw Jeff Thatcher, his face broke into a hopeful smile. But after looking at Jeff Thatcher's direction for some time, he again became morose and turned away in sorrow. When Jeff reached the schoolyard, Tom began

talking to him, hoping the boy would mention his sister, Becky Thatcher. But neither did Jeff mention Becky, nor could Tom see her anywhere in school. He became very upset indeed.

Then one day, Becky again began coming to school. It appeared that she was cured of whatever was the cause of her ailment. Tom was extremely happy when he saw her blonde hair and pretty face in the schoolyard. He tried to gain her attention by jumping over the fence, yelling, standing on his hands and staring at her. But despite trying every trick that he could think of, he did not succeed in attracting Becky's attention. She did not even look in his direction.

Tom was extremely embarrassed by her refusal to acknowledge him. He had made a fool of himself to please her but she completely ignored him.

Tom felt staying in school after such a disappointment was pointless. Feeling miserable, he packed his things and sneaked out of school when no one watching.

He kept walking farther and farther away from school until it looked like a tiny speck in the horizon. He was upset, ashamed and desperate. Nothing seemed to matter to his poor life anymore. He felt friendless and forsaken. It seemed to him that nobody would even care if he lived or died.

Tom was so upset and carried away by his misery that he did not notice his old friend, Joe Harper, coming towards him. Joe looked even sadder than Tom!

When Tom asked him what happened, he said that he had just been punished by his mother for drinking some cream but it was unfair because he never even touched it. He mournfully looked at Tom, swearing his complete innocence in the matter.

The two boys continued discussing the injustices done to them as they walked on. They decided to make an agreement to always support each other as brothers and never part from each other until death.

They started planning different ways to escape from their respective situations. Joe suggested that they turn into hermits and live impoverished lives in a remote cave, eating only rough bread and water. Tom, on the other hand, had a much more exciting idea. He said that they should become pirates!

Tom also knew of a perfect place for them to hide as pirates. It was a small, deserted island on the Mississippi river that no one lived in. It was called Jackson's Island.

Tom and Joe then searched for Huck and asked him to join them. To him, all careers were the same and he happily agreed to become a pirate.

When all three boys were ready for their wild adventure, they made plans to meet at an isolated spot on the riverbank, about two miles above the village. Each boy was supposed to bring fishing hooks, lines, sinkers and as much food, and other necessities as he could manage to steal. Having reached the decision, the boys parted ways.

It was a starry, quiet night. As Tom began walking away from the village towards their meeting spot, the huge Mississippi river seemed immobile and at peace — almost like a calm ocean. On reaching the bank, Tom could not at first see either Huck or Joe so he gave a long, low whistle, and the boys came out from behind some bushes where they were hiding.

The three boys had quite a bit of food amongst themselves. Joe brought a large portion of bacon, Huck had a skillet, a pouch of tobacco and some corncobs to make smoking pipes with, and Tom carried with him a several boiled ham cakes.

The boys had a small raft tied up on the bank and they loaded it with all the provisions. Finally, all set, they pushed the raft away from the bank and began sailing towards Jackson's Island.

The three boys on their raft reached Jackson's Island at about two o'clock that night. Jumping off it, they tied it to a tree truck and went looking for wood to light a fire.

They gathered firewood and built their fire against the side of a huge log. For dinner, they decided to roast some bacon. The bright fire lit up their faces as well as the surrounding trees and other flora.

When they had finished eating their dinner, the three happy pirates lay down on the grass and fell asleep without a care in the world. All three boys were very content.

When Tom woke up the next morning, it took him a while to remember where he was. Within a few minutes he recalled that he had run away from home and had come to Jackson's Island to become a pirate with Huck and Joe.

Huck and Joe were both still asleep. Tom hurriedly woke them up and they all began to talk together, excitedly. Very soon, they had all stripped off their clothing and were chasing one another in land and in the shallow waters near the island shore.

By the time they returned to their camp, they were refreshed, happy and very hungry. Soon,

they built another fire with the firewood that they had collected. Huck had caught a catfish in the river and the three boys had a delicious breakfast of coffee, bacon and fried catfish.

They ate till they could not eat any further and then, with very satisfied stomachs, decided to explore the island. They walked across it and discovered that it was about three miles long and one-fourth mile wide. A narrow channel of water, hardly hundred yards wide, separated the island from the shore that was closest to it.

Every hour the boys wanted to go swimming and what fun they had!

It was mid-afternoon by the time they decided that they had had enough swimming and returned to the camp.

They then had a large meal of cold ham and lay down to sleep. They talked of adventures and excitement, but soon realized that they were affected by the stillness and silence of the island. In short, they became lonely there all by themselves.

They were overwhelmed by the feeling of homesickness. Even Huck, who did not have a permanent home and usually slept in doorways and abandoned places, began to miss life in the village with its bustle and activity. Feeling quite ashamed of harbouring such emotions, the boys did not disclose their homesickness to one another and stayed silent.

Suddenly, in the distance, they heard a strange muffled boom. It was a peculiar sound and Tom shouted, "Let's go check it out!"

Springing quickly to their feet, the boys hurried towards the shore. They hid behind bushes and parted them to see what was happening. A little steam-boat was coming up the river. It was a mile above the village and its deck was crowded with people. A gigantic puff of white smoke burst out from the side of the boat and it was followed by the muffled booming sound that they had heard earlier.

"I know what's happening out there!" exclaimed Tom. "Somebody's drowned!"

Huck turned to Tom and said that he was right. The previous summer when Bill Turner had drowned, the same thing had taken place. Apparently, the people there believed that the boom could bring a drowned body to the surface of the water.

As they continued watching, Joe regretfully said, "I sure wish I was out there with those people. I wonder who drowned." He clearly missed being at the centre of all the excitement.

Standing still, they kept watching the little steam boat until suddenly Tom shouted that he knew who had drowned.

"It's us!" he yelled.

They were missing from the village and hence the search was for them. Instantly, each boy felt like a hero. They were missed. People mourned them. Their running away had caused heartbreaks. The entire village was talking about them. This was such a sweet victory! Being pirates, then, was indeed a worthwhile job.

As day gave way to evening, the little boat sailed back to dock and the little heroes returned to their camp, excited and delighted.

They discussed their triumph as they ate a dinner of fried fish which they had caught in the river. They mostly talked about who might be missing them and what people were saying about them.

When night finally descended upon them, they fell silent and stared at the fire. Tom and Joe kept thinking about the people back home who were missing them.

Joe was the first to broach the topic. Hesitatingly, he asked Huck and Tom how they would feel about returning to the village. They laughed at him for being silly and denied having any feeling of homesickness.

As the last embers of the fire burned away, the boys lay down to sleep but Tom could not fall asleep.

Chapter Eight

Tom Visits Home

Tom, being unable to sleep, waited till he was sure that both Huck and Joe had fallen off to sleep. When he was completely certain that they were sleeping soundly, he got up and walked carefully away from the camp, hiding behind trees and shrubs, towards the bank. When he had covered the distance between himself and the camp, he broke into a run and reached their little raft. Taking the raft, he paddled towards their village. When the current would not permit him to move any farther on the raft, he confidently entered the water and began swimming upstream.

He reached there by ten o'clock. He ran swiftly through the roads and lanes and finally reached Aunt Polly's backyard fence. He jumped over the fence and peeped inside. There was a light burning in the sitting room but no one seemed to be around. Tom went to the door and quickly opened it just enough for him to slip inside.

He cautiously entered Aunt Polly's bedroom and without making any sound slipped under her bed.

Soon after, Aunt Polly entered the room with another person and Tom began to eavesdrop on their conversation.

"He wasn't a bad boy at all, my Tom, only mischievous," cried Aunt Polly. "He never meant any harm to anyone and had such a large kind heart! And he was such a comfort to me."

She kept crying as she sat on the bed.

The other person, whom Tom recognized by her voice, was Joe's mother, Mrs. Harper. She, too, was sobbing, "That's just how my Joe was. Always up to some mischief but such a sweet, unselfish boy! I whipped him that day for stealing some cream, forgetting that I myself had thrown it out because it had gone sour."

Their words made Tom want to jump out from under the bed and console his mourners, but he kept himself calm and remained hidden.

Tom understood from their conversation that everybody in the village believed that the boys had drowned in the river while swimming. But when they heard of the stolen raft, they had become hopeful that the boys had probably just gone to the next village down the river. That hope too was dashed because they were not in any of the neighbouring villages. They believed that the boys had drowned somewhere in the middle of the river.

If the bodies were not retrieved by Saturday, then their funeral would be held at noon that Sunday.

Tom was horrified when he heard of his impending funeral. He watched helplessly as Aunt Polly knelt by her bed and prayed for him.

Her words of love and endearment for her poor drowned nephew affected him strongly.

After Mrs. Harper left, sobbing all the while, and Aunt Polly had gone off to sleep, Tom crept out of his hiding place and stood by the bed, looking at Aunt Polly by the light of a candle. She was moaning a little in her sleep as though dreaming about her missing nephew. He felt truly sympathetic towards her and decided to write a note to inform her that he was, in fact, alive and well and not dead.

Tom took out a piece of a tree's bark from his pocket. He put it on the table and was thinking of what he ought to write. Just as he was about to jot down the first word, an idea struck him and, smiling to himself, he put the bark back inside his pocket. He decided not to write anything at all.

Before leaving, he turned back towards his aunt and kissed her lightly. He had a plan and he knew he would be returning again very soon.

On his way back, Tom found the ferry boat that they had seen searching for them that

morning. He knew that watchman was fast asleep and so bravely climbed aboard and, untying her moorings, decided to row away towards Jackson's Island. He knew that when the boat was found missing a thorough search would be made for it, decided that since it might be considered a ship, it was a worthy prey for a pirate like himself. However, after much contemplation, he felt that they might be discovered if the boat was found on their island and so, though tempted to steal it, he left it alone and rowed back towards the island on the raft.

Chapter Nine

The Pirates Return

Tom had rested for a while on his way and so, by the time he reached back to the camp it was broad daylight. Huck and Joe were already awake and worriedly discussing his disappearance. They had just begun wondering what to do when Tom made his appearance. Over a scrumptious breakfast of bacon and fish that Huck and Joe had caught that morning, Tom told them all about his adventure, adding quite a few exciting touches to it. The three of them were a company of heroes! He then lay down in the shade of a tree and slept till noon.

That afternoon, the boys went hunting for turtle eggs. They would poke sticks in the sand

and wherever it was soft, they would kneel down and scoop out the eggs. They sometimes found fifty to sixty eggs in a single hole. The eggs were perfectly round and white and a little smaller than a walnut. They had quite a feast of fried egg that night.

The boys went swimming and fishing in the Mississippi waters until they were tired. They made a ring in the sand and played 'circus'. They took out their marbles and played 'knucks' and 'keeps' but soon got bored with all these games. Each boy was feeling sad and lonely as he looked across the river towards the home they had deserted.

Tom scribbled 'Becky' on the sand with his big toe, feeling homesick, but immediately scrubbed it off angrily, thinking that it was a weakness in a pirate. But he wrote it again and erased it again.

When the three boys rested, neither of them was feeling jolly. Joe felt so miserable that he nearly had tears in his eyes. Huck, a homeless kid, also missed the village. They sat quietly, each in his own thoughts.

It was Joe who finally said, "Let's stop being pirates now. It's so lonely here and I really miss my home."

Tom tried to cheer him up by telling him how wonderful the fishing was on the island.

"I don't care about fishing," cried Joe. "I want to go home."

"But Joe this is the best place for fishing. And think of all the fun we're having!" Tom tried to convince Joe. "And I'm sure there've been pirates here before. How'd you feel if we found a whole chest of treasures?"

Joe was still sorrowful. Tom tried telling him about the lovely swimming here which they could not have anywhere else but did not succeed in raising his spirits.

It was pointless. Even Huck, felt that it was time to go home. But Tom remained firm in his decision to stay on in the island.

By the time it grew dark, Huck and Joe started gathering their things. They did not want to leave Tom all alone, but he adamantly refused to follow them.

Finally, when all their packing was done, Huck and Joe were about to leave, and Huck told Tom that he still had time to think about his decision and join them. They would wait for him on the shore for some time.

As the two boys walked slowly away from Tom, he suddenly had a brilliant idea and ran towards them, yelling, "Stop! Wait! There's something I've got to tell you!"

Joe and Huck stopped and listened to Tom. As they listened, they began to get excited. Both boys agreed at once to Tom's plan, though it meant that they would have to stay in the island for a few more days. Tom's idea was that on Sunday, that is, the day of their funeral, the three boys would mysteriously rise from the dead and shock everyone.

Since now the boys knew that they would soon be going home, they spent the next four days with greater ease. The boys decided to home a lot of fun. They fished, swam and played games. They also made plans about

how they would surprise everyone with their return.

On Sunday, the whole village was silent and sorrowful. The Harpers and Aunt Polly's family were weeping and grieving their loss while the rest of the villagers had only one topic of discussion – the disappearance of the boys.

Even Becky Thatcher was depressed and paced across the empty schoolyard feeling lonely and muttering to herself.

"Oh if only I had not been so foolish as to return that brass doorknob," whispered Becky to herself. "I no longer have anything to remember him by."She sobbed, choked and wept. She wished she had not been so hard on Tom. "I'll never see him again!"

While tears rolled down Becky's cheeks, a group of boys sat in a corner and discussed about Tom and Joe. They were shocked that the two boys were really dead and would never come back. It was a difficult thing to accept.

At noon, which was the time for the funeral, the church bell began to toll and the villagers

gathered in the church. People were whispering to one another about the tragedy. The little church was completely packed with people.

As the mourners – Aunt Polly, Sid and the Harper family – entered the church, everybody became silent. The procession of mourners was dressed in black and everybody stood up, as a mark of respect, while they walked towards the aisle.

The priest who was presiding over the funeral sermon described each boy in wonderful terms. He spoke of several incidents which had happened in their lives and by the time his speech was over, nearly everyone who had gathered had tears in their eyes.

Everybody was so caught up in the priest's words that they did not notice the slight rustling sound coming from the gallery. Then the church door creaked open and to the amazement of all present, in walked the three boys.Everyone present in the church were shocked to see the three boys alive. Tom was leading, Joe followed next and Huck came in last.

The little runaways had hidden in the gallery and were listening to their own funeral sermon!

The boys were immediately engulfed in hugs and kisses by Aunt Polly and the Harper family. Even Huck, who had no family to mourn his death because his father was a drunkard and did not particularly care, was hugged by Aunt Polly, as she cried, "Poor motherless child!"

Huck was uncomfortable with the shower of affection on him because he was not used to being loved. But he too felt happy that somebody was glad to see him alive.

The priest suddenly shouted as loudly as he could, "Praise the Lord! Sing! Put your hearts in it!"

And while the whole church, full of people, began singing and praising the lord for the safe return of the three boys, Tom looked around at his friends and thought that they were jealous of the attention he was receiving. This was indeed a very proud moment for Tom Sawyer.

Chapter Ten

Back Home Again

It was all Tom's plan. He had wanted to become a pirate and then felt homesick, but could not show his fellow-pirates that he was weak. So he was the one who had planned to return home and listen to their own funeral sermon, and surprise everyone. In short, Tom was very proud of what he had done.

The next morning at breakfast, Tom was busy regaling Sid with tales of his adventures on the island, and how exciting it was to attend one's own funeral. Aunt Polly and Mary were also present and were very kind towards Tom.

After some time, though, Aunt Polly told Tom that it was not a very good thing to do, worrying

everyone so much, as though he did not care about them. "You made us all suffer so much only so you could have a good time."

She called him hard-hearted and said that if he could come back for the funeral then surely he could have found a way to let her know that he was alive and well. She said that he did not truly love her and only wanted to cause her sorrow by this kind of behaviour.

Mary pleaded on Tom's behalf, "He didn't think, Aunty. You know Tom. He just went in a rush and didn't think about the consequences."

"If Sid was in his place, he would surely have found a way to let me know," replied Aunt Polly. "Sid would have thought about his poor aunt."

Then she turned towards Tom and said, "When you grow up, perhaps someday you'll think about how little it would have cost you to care a little more for me and then it'll be too late."

These words made Tom feel very guilty about his actions. He was almost about to confess to

Aunt Polly that he had come to the village and almost left her a note, informing her that he was fine. But instead of owning up to the truth and making her feel better, he decided to create a fantastic lie about a dream that he had while on Jackson's Island.

He said that he had dreamed about Aunt Polly and the others on Wednesday night. That was the night he had come to see her but, of course, he did not tell her so.

"I dreamed that I was here in this very room, Aunty. And Joe Harper's mother was here too," said Tom convincingly. "It seems a little dim now after so long."

Aunt Polly urged him to think harder.

Tom agreed and then said that first he dreamed about was that something blew the candle in the room. This had actually happened on that night when Tom opened the door to enter and the wind blew inside. Aunt Polly had made Sid go and shut the door and Tom said that he saw that in his dream as well.

He then said that, in that very room, Mrs. Harper and Aunt Polly were weeping and discussing how they missed the two boys. He said that, in his dream, Aunt Polly was telling Mrs. Harper how Tom was kind and generous even when he was mischievous. In response, Mrs. Harper had replied that her son too was not bad but merely naughty and that she had wrongly whipped him for stealing cream that she herself had thrown away.

Tom's description of his dream was exactly what had happened there that fateful night. Aunt Polly was very surprised. She believed that some sort of good spirit was watching over Tom when he had run away. She also thought that he was special and gifted, and became so happy that she opened her cupboard, took a big, red, juicy apple from it and gave it to him to eat on his way to school.

In school, Tom had become a hero in the eyes of his classmates. He no longer ran or jumped or played cheerfully with his friends. Now he

walked in a reserved, solemn manner, with his head held high and thinking of himself as a great pirate!

His classmates flocked around him and villagers talked about him. Younger boys would surround him and be proud to be in his presence, while older boys grew jealous of him. Tom pretended not to notice that everybody spoke about him, Joe and their adventures. But in reality, he was extremely pleased with all the attention that he was getting.

It seemed as though every boy in the village wanted to please him and wished that they too had his deeply suntanned skin and fame.

All the admiration and flattering looks made Tom and Joe quite proud and vain. They felt superior to the other boys and repeatedly told all about their adventure to people who kept coming back to hear their delightful tale.

Tom became so proud of his status as a hero that he now believed that he did not need Becky Thatcher any more. Fame and glory were enough

to keep him satisfied. He expected her to come to him and try to make up for being rude. He decided that he would not accept her apologies, if she made any, and ignore her just as she had earlier ignored him.

When Becky came to school, Tom looked away as though he did not see her. He quickly joined a group of boys and girls and began talking to them. He noticed that she was running up and down the schoolyard, chasing her classmates, with bright shining eyes and a happy look. Though she was laughing as she played, she always seemed to be chasing only those who happened to be near Tom's group.

Quite a number of times, she came closer to his group, looking at him as though she wanted to say something, but every time Tom would be speaking to Amy Lawrence more than anyone else.

Becky grew very jealous. She wanted to move away from the group but, overcome by anger and envy, she walked over to them and announced that she would be having a picnic during vacation

and her mother had permitted her to invite anyone whom she wished to invite.

Her schoolmates became very excited and began asking her to invite them, and Becky happily told them that they were all invited.

However, only Tom and Amy did not ask her for an invitation. They turned their backs on her and walked off in a huff.

Becky was very disappointed and upset. She almost cried but managed to cover up her disappointment with fake laughter.

When she was alone, she hid herself and had a good cry. She then moodily decided to get even with Tom for upsetting her and hurting her pride.

At lunch break, Tom continued to laugh and have a good time with Amy Lawrence. He looked up to see if Becky was watching him and how she was affected. But, instead of seeing a sad and forlorn Becky, he saw that she was sitting cosily on a little bench with Alfred Temple, looking at a picture book. They seemed to be so interested in it that their heads were almost touching.

Tom became very jealous and blamed himself for being stupid and not accepting Becky's friendship when he had an opportunity. He did not really prefer Amy over Becky. At noon, he sneaked out of school and ran away to home. He could no longer bear to pretend to like Amy. Nor could he tolerate seeing Becky so happy with Alfred.

Of course, Becky was not interested in Alfred either. When Tom left, she saw that she had won the battle of who could hurt the other more, but she felt sad and depressed, and told Alfred that she no longer cared for his picture book. She left him and started crying.

Alfred ran after her, trying to understand what happened but she merely snapped at him, "Go away! I hate you!"

Alfred was really surprised but then he realized that Becky had simply used him to make Tom jealous. He became very angry that she had dared to humiliate him like that. He decided to make Tom pay. But he did not know how.

After much thinking, Alfred hit upon the perfect revenge plan. He went to the classroom and found Tom's spelling book on his desk. Seeing Tom nowhere around, Alfred spilled ink all over it.

What Alfred did not know was that Becky had seen him doing it from a window. But she chose not to say anything and moved away. She hoped to find Tom and tell him what she had seen Alfred doing and thus, make up with him by making him grateful to her.

But before Becky reached home, she changed her mind. She remembered how cruel Tom had been to her and decided to let him face the punishment for the spoiled spelling book.

Chapter Eleven

Aunt Polly Learns The Truth

Tom was in a very sad mood when he reached back home from school. But before he could say anything to his Aunt Polly, she looked at him fiercely and said, "Tom, I might just whip you and skin you alive for this!"

"But why, Aunt Polly?" asked Tom in surprise.

Aunt Polly looked at him angrily and said that she had gone to Joe Harper's house to tell his mother about Tom's wonderful dream and how accurate it was. Turns out, Joe had told his mother all about the night when Tom had taken the raft and come to the village and now, Aunt

Polly knew that he was there the whole time and it was no dream. Aunt Polly felt cheated.

"Tom, I don't know what to do with a naughty boy like you. I feel so horrible for making a fool of myself in front of Mrs. Harper."

Tom was very ashamed of what he had done and could barely look at his aunt's face. He mumbled that he did not expect her to find out about it. This made Aunt Polly even angrier. Tom then looked at her meekly and told her that he had returned that night because he knew she would be worried and he wanted to reassure her that he had not drowned and was alive and well.

"I don't believe you, Tom," said Aunt Polly. "It would be wonderful if you were such a thoughtful, caring boy but you did not have any such notion. You think about nothing but your selfishness."

She looked at him sternly. Tom begged her to believe that he was not lying. He told her that he come back the other night to tell her he was alive.

"But when I heard you and Mrs. Harper discussing our funeral, I got tempted to make a surprising scene. It seemed like such a super plan to come back and hide in the church gallery and surprise you all that I didn't want to spoil it by showing myself to you," replied Tom, feeling very downcast.

He then told Aunt Polly, "That's when I put the bark back in my pocket and decided to silently leave.

"What bark?" asked Aunt Polly.

"The bark on which I wrote to tell you that we were pirating!" he replied. "Now I wish you had woken up when I kissed you before leaving."

On hearing that Tom had kissed her before he left that night, mellowed Aunt Polly's anger. She looked at his young face and knew that he was telling the truth. She felt tender and loving towards Tom for this little streak of affection in him.

But she still had to be sure.

After sending Tom to school, Aunt Polly went to his cupboard and took out the jacket that he

had worn when he was on Jackson's Island, pirating. She could not decide at first whether or not to check his pockets or not because if she found out that he had been lying, she would be very upset. After hesitating twice, she finally put her hand in his pockets and in one of them, discovered the bark.

As she read the bark, Aunt Polly felt so happy with Tom that she decided she could forgive him for a million crimes. She knew that despite his mischievous streak, he did truly love her.

From then on, Aunt Polly's manner towards Tom changed somewhat, and her mellowness and kind smile made him light-hearted and happy again.

In school, when Tom met Becky Thatcher, he begged her to forgive him, saying, "I've been very mean. I won't ever be like that again. Please make up."

But Becky refused to forgive him, with the words, "Keep yourself to yourself, Mr. Tom

125

Sawyer." She tossed her hair and walked off in a huff.

Next time Tom met her, he made a rude remark to her. Becky responded with another rude statement. Now their enmity was at its peak and she could not wait to see Tom getting whipped for his spoiled spelling book.

But later that day, Becky committed the most serious crime of tearing a page of their teacher, Mr. Dobbin's book, by mistake. Tom had seen her doing it, and she was sure that he would complain to Mr. Dobbins about it and she would be in trouble.

However, that day in class Tom felt sorry for Becky when he saw her trembling under the gaze of Mr. Dobbins, and despite telling himself that her punishment would mean nothing to him, he stood up and claimed to have committed the crime.

He got whipped mercilessly for it, but he bore it all without a sound. He did not quite understand what made him rush to Becky's

defence like that. Later that day, she was waiting for him outside the school gate and confessed that she had witnessed Alfred Temple spoiling Tom's spelling-book. She was ashamed that she had not told the truth in class.

Then she exclaimed, "Tom, how could you be so noble?"

By the time he reached home, Tom forgot all about the beatings and only remembered Becky's kind words and how she had called him noble!

Chapter Twelve

The Salvation Of Muff Potter

Summer break came soon and brought with it fun as well as disappointment for the boys. Unfortunately for poor Tom, he managed to catch measles and had to stay in bed for almost three weeks. Those three weeks felt like an eternity to Tom who could not wait to go out and play and have fun with his friends. When he was finally cured and allowed to go outside, there was a lot of excitement in the village.

The cause of the excitement was Muff Potter's trial was just about to begin. Everybody talked about the trial and wherever Tom went, somebody or the other was surely discussing its nature and possibility of outcome.

Whenever Tom heard of the trial, he began sweating and trembling, despite the heat. He was not only frightened but also feeling very guilty about hiding a secret that could save an innocent man's life.

At last, when he could no longer stand the constant pricking of his conscience, he went looking for Huck. He felt that by talking to Huck about it, he could unburden his guilty feeling. He also wanted to make sure that Huck had not told anyone about that night.

So, when he found Huck, he asked him, "Have you told anyone?"

"Told what?" asked Huck.

"About you-know-what," replied Tom frustrated.

"Of course not!"

"Not a single word to anyone?"

"It's God's honest truth," replied Huck, "that I've told no one about it."

Tom believed Huck and the two boys decided to reseal their oath. So again they pricked their

fingers and swore over their blood to never reveal what had happened that night.

Then they began discussing Muff's fate.

"People were saying that they'll take action against Muff if the court frees him," said Tom, worriedly.

The boys walked and talked together for a long time, discussing various things, but they were both feeling guilty about their action. It was early evening when they reached the neighbourhood of the prison. Though the boys desperately hoped for something to happen that would save Muff's life, they knew that only they could help him.

All that they could do was sneak some tobacco and matches to Muff through the tiny window of the prison. But Muff seemed so grateful with these little gifts that the boys felt even more guilty.

When Tom went home after visiting Muff, He was feeling horrible and had nightmares that night.

Every day, during the trial, Tom waited outside the courtroom. He was being pulled apart from inside by his desire to help Muff and his fear of

Injun Joe as well as the blood-oath he had taken with Huck.

Huck, too, could not summon the courage to enter the courtroom and waited outside.

Then came the last day of the trial. The judge and jury arrived and took their seats. All the villagers were eagerly waiting for the outcome of the trial.

Soon, Muff was brought into the courtroom. He looked pale, sad, unwell and there was a sort of hopelessness in the way he walked and looked. Everybody was looking at him. Injun Joe was also present in the courtroom and had a fierce, angry and hateful expression on his face.

Muff's lawyer stood up to face the jury, before they could announce their judgment, and said that he had an important witness. He changed Muff's plea to 'not-guilty'.

Loudly and clearly, the lawyer said, "Call Tom Sawyer to the witness stand."

That day Tom was present inside the courtroom. Everybody turned in their seats, with puzzled looks, as Tom stood up and walked to the witness

stand. Tom was very frightened but faced his fear and took the oath without hesitation.

"Tom Sawyer," asked Muff's lawyer, "where were you around midnight on the seventeenth of June?"

Tom was about to reply when he saw Injun Joe's face in the crowd and froze. He was so frightened by Joe's look that he could not utter a single word.

He then gulped and took a few deep breaths, and began telling his story. He did not omit anything and told it from the beginning to the end. He gave the details of the terrible murder. Tom also told the jury why he and Huck were in the cemetery that night.

As Tom told his story, Injun Joe knew that he was in trouble. So he jumped out of his seat, ran through the crowd, leapt across the window and disappeared before anybody could catch him.

Muff was set free because of Tom's testimony.

But Tom knew that Injun Joe was alive and waiting somewhere for his revenge.

Chapter Thirteen

Digging For The Buried Treasure

Tom was a hero again! His name even appeared in a local newspaper. His fame and popularity made him extremely happy. He had a status to brag about in the village.

But at night, Tom could hardly sleep because of nightmares of Injun Joe. He was very frightened though he tried not to show it. He did not even go out to meet Huck anymore. Huck was also as scared as Tom.

The night before the jury was to declare its verdict, Tom had gone to meet Muff's attorney. He confessed everything. Huck was annoyed and angry with Tom for breaking their oath,

but Tom could no longer bear the burden of his guilty conscience.

Now that the villain had escaped, both Huck and Tom were equally frightened. Every moment they felt that Injun Joe would hunt them down and punish them for disclosing his secret. They knew that they would not be safe until he was captured and safely imprisoned or dead.

There were posters put up in every nearby town and village declaring a reward for Injun Joe's capture but no news could be found. A detective was also hired to find him but Injun Joe's whereabouts remained unknown.

As time passed and the days went on, Tom and Huck began to be less and less frightened. They were adventurous boys and soon forgot all about the trial and got back to their old sports.

One day, Tom told Huck that they should dig for buried treasure. Huck was not so sure about the idea but Tom told him that there was treasure buried everywhere and one just needed to dig to find them. He told poor illiterate Huck stories of

robbers who hid their stolen loot in abandoned houses and under dead trees. He was so good with his words, which he had picked up from adventure books that he had read, that Huck finally agreed to join him and dig for treasure.

They walked three miles to Still-House Hill, carrying shovels and picks. When they saw a dead tree, they started digging. The boys sweated and toiled for an hour, digging with much expectation, but could find no treasure.

"Do robbers bury their treasure so deep?" asked Huck.

"Sometimes," replied Tom. "Maybe we're just digging under the wrong tree."

They quit digging under that tree and walked on. They came across another dead tree and began digging under it too. After they had dug for a long time, under several trees, the boys soon became very tired.

That's when Tom got another of his brilliant ideas. "Let's look in the haunted house Cardiff Hill!" he said with shining eyes.

Huck said that they would be in trouble as it was haunted. But Tom convinced him by saying that people only thought it was haunted because it was abandoned. No one was brave enough to explore it. He was certain that they would find treasure in it.

When they reached the house, the unearthly silence, cobwebs, floorless rooms with overgrown weed and windows missing their panes frightened the boys very much.

They entered quietly and, moving forward, found an old closet. Feeling scared and also curious, they turned the knob to open the closet. It was empty.

This encouraged the boys and they moved towards the second floor. Just when they reached the top of the stairs, they heard a noise.

"What is that?" whispered Tom.

They heard it again.

"Let's run!" whispered Huck, fearfully.

But they could not run because any noise would alert whoever was there to their presence.

So they lay down on the floor, trying to see through the rotting wood, shuddering in fear.

Two men entered the house. One was an old deaf-and-dumb beggar who had recently come to their village. They could not recognize the other man who was dressed shabbily and had unkempt hair.

The two began to talk. The second man's voice seemed familiar to the boys.

The beggar, who was neither deaf nor dumb, was saying, "It's not a dangerous job. Do it!"

The boys were shocked to see the deaf-and-dumb man speak. Then they recognized the ragged man's voice. It was none other than Injun Joe!

The boys froze, barely daring to breathe.

The two men chatted for a while, ate their lunch and then slept. That is when Huck and Tom thought that they could escape. They began to crawl forward and moved towards the staircase. But the first step they took made such a loud

creaking noise on the floor that they became weak with fear and sat down.

Thankfully, the noise went unheard by the two men downstairs.

After some time, Injun Joe woke up. He stood up and kicked his partner on his chest to wake him up.

The two men began counting their money. They had six hundred dollars which they decided to hide in that very room until they could find a way to escape undetected. Injun Joe began tearing apart floorboards with his knife and hands, to hide their money, when he found an old rusty box.

"What's this?" muttered Injun Joe and opened the box.

They exclaimed loudly when they saw what was in the box. It was full of gold coins and money worth thousands of dollars! They found a treasure chest!

"What luck!" shouted Injun Joe's partner. "Now we can forget about the other job. We're rich!"

But Injun Joe looked at him and said, "That job is for my revenge. It's not just a robbery. I need your help with it and then we can leave this place with all the money."

The moment they heard him speaking of 'revenge' the boys began to tremble. He was surely after them for betraying his secret at Muff's trial.

Injun Joe and his partner then decided to bury the treasure.

"I'll bury it under the cross, at number two," said the beggar and they both left with their shovels and picks and the treasure box.

The two men did not return. Huck and Tom waited for a long time before coming out of their hiding place. They could think of nothing else on their way home apart from Injun Joe's revenge and the buried treasure.

Chapter Fourteen

Trembling On The Trail

Since that eventful day in the abandoned house, all Tom could think of was Injun Joe's revenge and the money that they had seen. In fact, his dreams were also full of the wonderful treasure that he and Huck had seen. Tom never knew till that day that so much money could even exist. If only they could understand what the beggar had meant by "under the cross, at number two," he and Huck would be able to have all that treasure.

The day after overhearing Injun Joe and his partner, Tom met Huck beside the river to make plans on what to do and how. Tom wanted to get his hands on the treasure. He was very excited

about how Huck and he could actually take it away from the bad men.

At first, Huck was not very sure if they could deceive Injun Joe and the beggar, and take the treasure. He felt that a person only gets one chance to grab so much money and theirs was gone.

But Tom refused to accept defeat so easily. He was very keen to find the treasure and enjoy this wonderful adventure that seemed to have almost been forced upon them.

Huck was no less adventurous and finally said, "Ok, sure, but what's this 'number two'? I don't think it's a house number 'coz houses in our village don't have numbers."

After much thinking, Tom said that it was possible for "number two" to be the number of a room in an inn.

Huck agreed with Tom. There were only two inns in the village and it would be easy to find out which one had a room numbered two. Tom's idea seemed quite reasonable to Huck, so Tom told him to wait there while he went and collected the information.

Leaving Huck by the riverbank, Tom ran towards the inns in the village and returned within an hour. He was very excited because he had an important piece of news. The bigger inn had a room numbered 'two' which was occupied by a lawyer. But the smaller inn also had a room numbered two. The innkeeper's son had told Tom that room number two was kept locked all the time. Apparently it was haunted, as he told Tom, and that he had seen a light shining in that room the night before.

Tom was sure that this must be the room that Injun Joe and the beggar had meant in the abandoned house, when they said "number two".

The boys decided to check out the place and find out whatever they could about it.

That night, Tom slipped out of his house and the two boys hid outside the smaller inn, close to its front door. They waited for several hours but neither Injun Joe nor his partner turned up. Both boys were disappointed but decided to come back and keep watch again the next night.

The next night, again, the two boys met and began to keep watch over the inn's door. Telling Huck to wait in the shadows, Tom decided to move forward and slowly crept towards the door holding a dimly lit lantern.

Huck silently waited, without getting a single glimpse of his friend or the lantern's light, for what seemed to be quite a few hours. He began to get very worried. It was only a few minutes in reality but time was stretched in Huck's frightened imagination.

"What if he fainted?" Huck wondered. "Or if he's caught? Oh Lord, I hope he isn't dead!"

Huck sat shivering in his hiding spot and was feeling very scared and concerned about Tom when suddenly, almost like a bolt of lightning, Tom came running towards him, yelling, "Run, Huck! Run for your life!"

Next moment Tom was running past Huck, he was so fast!

Huck did not need another warning. He got up at once and began to follow Tom. They kept

running till they reached an abandoned slaughter-house at the lower end of the village. They just managed to enter it when it began raining heavily and thunder and lightning filled the night sky.

After breathing heavily for some time, Tom calmed down enough to tell Huck what had happened.

"I tried to pick the lock and open the door but the lock seemed to be jammed. Then, without thinking, I just turned the doorknob and what do you think happened? The door was unlocked and it opened. And I jumped in. And guess what? I nearly stepped on Injun Joe's hand!"

"No!" cried Huck, horrified.

"Yes!" replied Tom. "He was lying there, on the floor, with his arms spread. He was completely drunk."

"Did he wake up?"

"No, he didn't even move a little. And Huck, I didn't see either the box or a cross. There were two barrels and lots of bottles in the room. Injun Joe is so drunk now, I think it's a good time to

go and grab the box if it's somewhere there and I just didn't notice!"

But the boys realized that neither of them had enough courage left to go back to the inn. Instead, they decided to continue keep a watch over it. Huck, who had no home to return to at night, would stand guard and if he saw Injun Joe or his partner leave the inn, he would go and call Tom.

"I'll keep watch every night," said Huck, "if you go in and grab the box the night they're not around."

Tom agreed.

The storm had passed by then and the boys bade each other goodbye. It would be dawn in a couple of hours.

That night, Huck slept in a deserted barn.

Tom went home, sneaked in through the window, and went to bed. All night long, he could only think about the hidden treasure and Injun Joe's face. Later, when he slept, he dreamed of them.

Chapter Fifteen

Huck Saves The Widow

The next morning Tom got a piece of very good news. Becky Thatcher and her family, who had been out on vacation, had just returned to the village. Immediately, Tom forgot all about Injun Joe and the hidden treasure and began thinking of Becky. He was very excited to meet her.

He went to meet her at once and the two of them spent the whole afternoon talking and playing games. Becky managed to get her mother's permission for the picnic that she had spoken of long time ago. It was planned for the next day, and invitations were sent out to all their friends before evening. All the boys and girls

were looking forward to the picnic as it was sure to be a lot of fun!

When Tom went to bed that night, though, he was not thinking about the picnic or about Becky, but waiting eagerly for Huck's call, "meow", from outside. But he was disappointed because Huck did not come. After waiting for a long time, Tom finally fell asleep.

The next day, Tom, Becky and all their friends got up early and gathered at the Thatchers' house for the picnic. When everyone was present, they went to the riverbank and boarded a little ferryboat and sailed towards the other bank of the river.

The boat stopped about three miles downstream from the village and everybody got out and began enjoying the picnic. It was a small clearing in the forest. Soon, the shouts and laughter of the children could be heard from miles away.

In the midst of so much fun, somebody shouted, "Who's ready for the cave?"

There was a loud and happy answer, "Yeah!" and they took out candles and began walking towards the opening of a cave.

The cave looked like a giant mouth of rock, shaped like the letter 'A'. Inside the opening was a small chamber which was very cold and covered with limestone. The cave, with its darkness and solemnity, seemed like a place of mystery and romance. The first small chamber led to many criss-crossing passages and it was believed that if anyone got lost in any one of those passages and tunnels, then it could be days before he'd find his way out; or sometimes never manage to escape from the cave.

The cave was never fully explored and so, it was not mapped. There were several young people who knew some portions of it and no one dared to venture any further than a few steps into it. Tom knew as much about the cave as anyone else, which meant, he knew very little about it indeed.

The crowd of boys and girls entered the cave and began exploring it. They laughed and shouted but did not enter too deep into the fearsome cave. They passed almost an hour in this manner and then the ferryboat's bell rang and they knew their time was up. They ran out of the cave and raced towards the boat.

While the other children were returning to the village from their picnic, Huck was still standing guard behind a bush, close to the inn's door. He nearly lost hope of seeing Injun Joe or the beggar that day.

Then suddenly, he noticed two men hurrying past his hiding place. One of the men had a box under his arm.

"It's the box of treasure," thought Huck. "They're moving the treasure to some other place."

Huck knew that if he went to fetch Tom now, he would lose track of Injun Joe and his partner. He could not afford to waste any time now. He had to stop those bad men from running away with the treasure. But how?

The two men walked three blocks up the street and then turned left, at the foot of a low

hill. They kept walking and Huck followed them, maintaining a good distance from them so as not to get caught. Finally the men stopped. Huck saw that they were on the path that led to Widow Douglas's house.

Huck slowly moved closer to the men and hid himself so that he could hear their words without being discovered.

"Drat!" whispered Injun Joe, "she's got lights on. I think she's not alone. Someone must have come to visit her."

His partner said that they ought to leave in that case but Injun Joe refused. Then Huck understood that the that Injun Joe had spoken about was meant for Widow Douglas.

The Widow's dead husband was a judge, and once he had Injun Joe whipped in front of everyone as a punishment for being a vagabond. Injun Joe never forgot that insult and had come to take revenge on Widow Douglas. He did not plan to kill her but make her suffer and, as he explained to his partner all the horrible things that he would do to torture her, he began polishing his knife.

Huck realized that he was again about to witness a crime and his first thought was to run away, unnoticed. But then he remembered that Widow Douglas had been kind to him many times, and he could not just watch her being tortured, or worse, murdered by these cruel men. But how could he inform her that she was in trouble? Huck finally decided upon his course of action. He very quietly slipped away from where he was hiding and softly began walking in the opposite direction from the one he had come. He then ran very fast to the nearest house and banged on their door. It was the house of Bill Welsh and his grown-up sons.

"Open the door! I'm Huckleberry Finn!"

"Who's that?" responded the old man. "What do you want?"

"Please," Huck nearly cried, "open the door and I'll tell you everything."

When Mr. Welsh opened the door, Huck tumbled in and breathlessly said, "Please don't tell that I told you… please… or he'll kill me!"

After that, Huck told the three men about Injun Joe hiding near Widow Douglas's house, planning to get his revenge by hurting and then maybe killing her. He told them to hurry up and save her before something horrible happened.

Mr. Welsh and his sons immediately took out their guns and ran towards the hill where Widow Douglas' house was situated. Huck did not go any farther with them. He sat motionlessly behind a huge rock and listened, trying to understand what was happening.

At first there was only silence. Then he heard gunshots. This was followed by a loud cry of pain by someone.

Huck could not tolerate it any longer and getting up from behind the rock, he ran down the hill as fast as he could, without turning back even once.

The next morning, Huck waited for the sun to rise and went at once to Mr. Welsh's house. All

three men were very pleased to see Huck and welcomed him in. They offered him breakfast and told him that though they had managed to save Widow Douglas, the villains had escaped. They nearly got Injun Joe and his partner, but unfortunately, Mr. Welsh sneezed loudly just as they were about to pounce on the two and hence, they were alerted and escaped.

They would not manage to go too far, though, because sentries and policemen had been placed all over the nearby villages and the riverbank to stop them form escaping.

Mr. Welsh also told Huck that they had found the box that the two men were carrying. Huck nearly fell off his chair in shock but managed to ask, "What was in it, Sir?"

"Tools, of course," replied Mr. Welsh. "Burglar's tools." He looked surprised that Huck would be so affected by the news of a box of tools.

So Huck knew that Injun Joe and the beggar had not moved the treasure. Where was it then?

Chapter Sixteen

Lost In The Cave

While all the excitement was going on with Huck, it went unnoticed that Tom and Becky were missing. They had gone exploring the other side of the cave and were too far away to hear the boat's bell. They did not know when everyone left. There were so many people boarding the boat all at once in time evening that in the laughter, and confusion and the darkness, nobody noticed that Tom and Becky were not with them.

Tom and Becky were quite lost as they had gone further and in a different direction from the rest of the picnickers. They walked through dark, long corridors, crossed round openings

to other tunnels and walked quite a distance, trying to recognie the path through which they had come.

Every time, they would end up in a different place. They got further lost by trying out different paths. Tom could not recognize a single tunnel as one that they had used before and he began losing his confidence.

Becky started crying.

"We're lost, Tom. We'll never get out of this maze of tunnels. We'll die here and no one will ever find us," she sobbed inconsolably.

Tom was not feeling too optimistic himself, but tried to calm her down by saying that they'd soon find a way out.

They walked through the tunnels and caverns for a long time and finally, growing very hungry, tired and dejected, they sat down and ate their last piece of cake. Now they had no food left. Their last candle was finally over and they were lost, sad and very scared. Becky could not walk any farther. Tom was silently worried and the darkness which covered them seemed to hang heavily upon them.

They talked of their families, friends, homes and comfortable beds. They fell asleep and woke up quite a number of times. They had no idea of time and could not even tell if it was night or day outside. They were both very hungry and were able to understand the continuous passage of time by their ever-increasing hunger.

"Will they miss us?" asked Becky finally. "Do you think they'll send people to look for us, Tom?"

"Of course, they will," Tom told her. He did not know whether he believed himself but tried to sound strong and confident for her.

They both knew that their families would be worried about them, but how much longer would they have to wait till they were rescued? Were their families aware that at the moment, the two of them were missing? Neither Tom, nor Becky could think of anything more to say and they both became silent.

Several hours passed. They were so hungry that they grew weak and hardly moved. Then Tom heard something.

"Shh!" he whispered. "Listen!"

They were motionless and even held their breaths to listen. There was a sound, far far away. It sounded like people were shouting.

Tom jumped to his feet and shouted back in reply. He then helped Becky get back on her feet. The two began slowly walking towards the direction of the sound. The darkness made it very difficult for them. Tom held Becky's hand as he led her forward. They stopped every few minutes to listen. The sound seemed to be getting closer and closer.

"We'll be saved now, Becky!" exclaimed Tom, delightedly. "People have come to rescue us."

Though they were still very hungry and tired, this new ray of hope gave them strength to keep moving forward. They moved slowly in the darkness. There were many pits on their path which slowed their progress even more.

Suddenly, they came across a pit which was very deep. They could not tell if it was three feet or a hundred feet deep. Tom lay down on his stomach and tired but could not touch the bottom of this pit. Whatever the exact depth might be, there was surely no crossing it.

They decided to wait there till the rescuers discovered them. But the voices began to grow fainter. The rescuers were trying a different direction now. Finally, they could no longer hear the voices.

Tom tried to attract their attention by shouting as loudly as he could. He shouted and shouted, but got no response. They were alone again. So they decided to move backward towards a freshwater spring which they had crossed on the way. There, they drank water and refreshed themselves and then lay down to rest.

When Tom woke up, he started thinking more clearly. He knew that it would be of no use to just sit there and do nothing. He also knew that there were narrow passages along the sides of

the tunnels. He had a ball of kite string in his pocket. He took the string, tied one end of it to a rock and began moving forward with Becky, unwinding the string slowly. They could retrace their steps to the spring if they got lost, by following the string.

Tom and Becky walked some twenty feet, when the tunnel ended in an outward bulge. Tom kneeled down, put his hands under it and looked out. He nearly jumped with joy! Not even twenty yards away from where they were, he saw someone's hand holding a candle.

Tom stood up and yelled happily. The moment he shouted, he saw the body and face of the person to whom the hand belonged. It was Injun Joe!

Injun Joe heard Tom's voice but did not recognize it. He just turned around in shock and fear and ran into the darkness.

Tom nearly fainted out of fright. He decided to follow the kite string back to the spring and stay there. He could not dare to face Injun Joe again.

Tom did not want to scare Becky and told her that he had only shouted for luck.

The two children went back to the spring and slept. They were very exhausted and Becky almost fainted out of hunger and tiredness. Tom was also feeling very weak and hungry but decided to look for some other way out of the maze of tunnels.

By this time, Becky believed that she was dying. She could neither speak properly nor sit up. She begged Tom to stay with her and hold her hand as she died and then use his kite string to find another way out of the cave.

Tom was heartbroken and distressed. He pretended to be sure that help was on the way but he too could not carry on much longer, having eaten no food for nearly three days.

He tried using the kite string one last time. Tying it to a rock, he crawled on his hands and knees towards a passage, desperate for a way to escape.

Chapter Seventeen

Escape!

In the village, everybody was mourning Tom and Becky's disappearance. They were gone for three days now and most people stopped searching for them and had resumed their everyday life. They were sure that the two children would never be found again.

Mrs. Thatcher became very ill. She was barely conscious. She would just lie in bed and weep. Sometimes she would call Becky's name, raise her head and try to listen for a response for a whole minute. She would then fall back into her pillow in exhaustion.

Aunt Polly also lost her spirit. Her hair which was gray, had turned almost completely white in those three days. She was constantly worried and upset.

All the people in the village seemed to be sad and downcast.

On Tuesday evening, the third day from the day of the picnic, when Tom and Becky went missing, the villagers sadly went to bed, talking about the two children.

At midnight, the village bells started ringing loudly. Everybody woke up and went to see what the matter was.

Soon the streets were full of people, half-asleep, half-dressed, but very happy, shouting excitedly, "They've been found! The kids have been found!"

People began banging tin pans and pails and other utensils as they all gathered near the bank of the river. Soon, a carriage came in, carrying Tom and Becky. The villagers took the two children in their arms. They were taken to Judge Thatcher's house to be nursed and taken care of and nearly everybody tried to touch them, kiss them or show them there offection in some other way. But nobody could speak much as they were all crying with relief and joy. This was probably the happiest day the little village had ever witnessed.

Aunt Polly was so happy that she could not describe her joy in words. She wept and smiled and could not take her eyes off Tom.

As for Mrs. Thatcher, she was waiting for her husband, who was still searching for the lost children at the cave, to receive her message that they had reached safely and soundly.

Tom, once again the centre of attention, lay down on a sofa surrounded by an audience that was very eager to hear his latest adventure. He told his tale, adding little snippets here and there to make it sound more exciting and described how, on the third day, he had left Becky who was almost unconscious and gone exploring by himself. He had followed two passages as far as his kite string would allow him to and reached dead-ends.

The third passage that he tried, however, turned out to be the lucky one. The length of his kite string had ended and he was about to turn back, disappointed, when he happened to see a glimpse of sunshine. He immediately dropped the string and crawled towards it and the first thing he saw was the Mississippi river flowing not far from where he was. He pushed his head and shoulders out to properly inspect the scene and then rushed back to get Becky.

Becky at first refused to believe him. She thought he was lying and was only trying to make her feel better.

"I'm about to die and I know it," she told Tom. She was very tired but Tom persisted with his good news. He finally managed to convince her that he was indeed telling her the truth and that they would now be saved. When he took her to the opening, Becky nearly died of joy. And that is how Tom and Becky managed to survive and return to the village.

"Imagine," said Tom, "if it had been night and I wasn't able to see the speck of daylight!"

Tom and Becky climbed out of the cave with some difficulty and sat there waiting for someone to notice them. They were both crying with happiness. Finally some men noticed the two children. They did not, at first, believe the strange tale that Tom told them. It seemed too improbable. But they were kind men and took the children home, fed them and let them sleep for some time before bringing them back to the village in a carriage.

This was the basic story, of course, but Tom made it so much more interesting by adding certain things here and embellishing other things there that he captured his audience's attention for a long time.

Three days of hunger and exhaustion made both Tom and Becky very weak. They both looked tired and pale and hardly ventured out of bed. Tom began walking a little by Thursday and was back to his own self by Saturday. Becky stayed

in bed till Sunday and despite resting so much, looked as though she had just recovered from a horrible illness.

Tom soon came to know that Huck was also unwell. He was staying with Mr. Welsh and his sons and was being taken care of by Widow Douglas. When he went to visit his friend, Widow Douglas told him about the night Huck had saved her and how it made him sick with all the fear and shock. She also told him not to upset Huck by mentioning the incident or anything related to it.

Tom already knew about the incident of that night. He was also told that one of the men, the deaf-and-dumb beggar who was neither deaf nor dumb, had drowned in the river while trying to escape. His body had been recently recovered floating on the river.

Tom went to visit Becky in her house about two weeks after their return. Mr. Thatcher was there with some of his friends. Keeping everybody's

safety in mind, Mr. Thatcher had decided to seal the cave and place it under triple lock.

The moment Tom heard it, he became pale and could not speak.

"What's wrong?" asked Mr. Thatcher in panic. "Someone run and get a glass of water for Tom. Quick!"

When water was brought and splashed on Tom's face, he regained some of his composure and, looking horrified, whispered, "Sir, Injun Joe is in the cave."

Chapter Eighteen

Buried Treasure

Tom's report about Injun Joe being stuck in the cave was soon known by everyone in the village. Within a few minutes, a few men and went to the cave with Tom and Mr. Thatcher.

When they reached the cave opening, which was sealed shut, they broke the locks and the door. The first thing that they saw was made them very sad indeed. Injun Joe was lying flat on the ground, motionless, with his face towards the door. There was a slight crack and perhaps that was what he had been looking at in his final moments before dying.

Injun Joe's life had been filled with darkness and he also died in the darkness of the cave, starving, friendless and alone.

Tom, who had spent three days in the cave, knew what Injun Joe must have suffered all these days locked up and without food, water or light. Tom felt very sad for the dead man. But more than that, he felt a sense of relief. He could now be free from the fear that he had been harbouring all these days.

Injun Joe was dead. He could no longer harm Tom or those he loved. Now, Tom would stop having the dreadful nightmares about him and his revenge. It was all over and he could roam about freely, without being scared all the time.

Injun Joe had a knife and it was found close to his body. The knife's blade was broken. It seemed to those present that he had spent his time stuck in the cave, trying to cut and break the door that blocked the cave's exit. His efforts had been in vain because the door was made of solid wood and was supported by blocks of rock. Injun Joe, who had avoided prison by running away, died in Nature's prison.

The cave, which was often visited by tourists, would normally have stubs of candle stuck on jutting out bits of rock or in hollows in the walls. There was no candle in sight when the men broke open the door. Injun Joe had taken whatever little piece of candle he could find and ate them. There were some claws on the floor of the cave. It seemed that he had also caught bats and eaten them to allay his hunger. Tom was horrified to see how the man had slowly starved to death.

He did not have Tom and Becky's good fortune to find a fresh water spring. So he had tried to collect drops of water from a stalactite on the roof of the cave. This must have been very frustrating because tiny drops of water would fall on the hollow piece of stone that Injun Joe had placed beneath the stalactite, after a long wait of three minutes between each drop.

Injun Joe was buried by the men near the opening of the cave. People came to see the site from several villages and towns. The news had spread and they all wanted to know what had happened and where. These people, with their lack of sympathy, almost made this sad event look like a picnic!

The next morning, Tom and Huck met on a hilltop to discuss in detail what all had happened to each of them. Mr. Welsh and Widow Douglas had told Huck everything about Tom's adventure. It was time for Huck to tell Tom about the things that had happened to him when Tom was gone.

Tom listened with rapt attention, as the other boy told him how he had been waiting for Injun Joe and his partner outside the inn.

"When they came out, I decided to follow them," said Huck.

He then told Tom how he had overheard them talking and came to know about their plan.

"I then ran to the Welshes' house as fast as I could, making sure that Injun Joe and his partner didn't realie that I was there. I begged Mr. Welsh to save Widow Douglas and off he went with his sons, carrying guns!"

When Tom heard everything, he told Huck, "You did a very brave thing. And it was right. But why didn't you want anyone to know that it was you who had saved the widow?"

"I was scared," replied Huck. "Widow Douglas was safe, sure, but Injun Joe had escaped."

Tom understood exactly how Huck had felt. He too had felt the same fear when he gave testimony to save Muff.

But this was all over now. Tom was eager to discuss something else with Huck — the treasure!

"Huck!" said Tom excitedly, "the money wasn't ever in room two of the inn!"

"What d'you mean?" asked Huck. "Have you found another clue to the treasure?" Huck's eyes lit up.

Tom replied, with a glint in his eyes, "It's in the cave!"

"What?" Huck was shocked. "Say that again."

"Huck," said Tom, "that money is in the cave!"

Huck refused to believe Tom at first but Tom swore that he was telling the truth.

The two boys immediately decided to go to the cave and search for it.

"But we won't get lost, will we?" asked Huck.

"No," answered Tom. "We'll take kite strings with us. Lots of them! And by using them, we won't get lost. We also need to take some food and bags to carry the treasure in. And we shouldn't forget matchsticks."

Without wasting any time, the two boys collected everything that they would need and started towards the cave. They stole a boat when its owner was not around. It was about half past noon, when the two boys reached the other side of the river. Tom showed Huck a small white mark that he had made on a slope of a hill. There was a tiny opening to the cave from there that no one knew about. Since the main mouth of the cave had been sealed shut, they had no option but to sneak in.

The hole that the two boys would enter through was very small and hidden behind bushes. If Tom

had not marked it, they would never have found it. Huck was very impressed.

They entered the cave through the little hole. Tom was leading while Huck followed. They went to the farthest end of the tunnel, slowly unwinding the kite strings. Memories of how he and Becky had suffered came back to him and he shuddered. He showed Huck a little stub of candle that had flickered and died, leaving him and Becky in darkness, as they lost their hopes and grew weak.

The boys continued moving forward, whispering softly to each other. Finally, Tom raised his candle high and pulled Huck's sleeve, saying, "Now you've got to see something. Do you see that big rock over there?" Tom pointed to a big rock on which something was scribbled with ash.

"It's a cross!" gasped Huck.

"And where's number two, do you think? Under the cross, of course!"

Huck speechlessly stared at the rock and the cross marked on it. Then he turned to Tom and whispered, "Let's leave. We gotta go from here."

When Tom asked why, Huck replied that the treasure belonged to Injun Joe and now that he was dead, his ghost would be guarding it. It must be nearby!

Tom told Huck that since they had found the treasure, it now belonged to them.

"And there can't be any ghost around here, Huck. Don't you know that the cross is a holy symbol and ghosts never come near them? And anyway, we've both suffered so much for it. We can't just let it go like that now."

Huck saw the point in Tom's words and the boys moved closer to the rock.

At the foot of the rock, they found a blanket, some tools and a piece of spoilt meat. There was no treasure!

"It's 'under' the cross," said Tom.

"But the rock is solidly set on the floor," replied Huck. "The treasure can't be under it, Tom."

The two boys searched all around the rock but could find absolutely nothing. They grew sad and disappointed and sat down. While Huck felt sorry for himself and his friend, Tom was thinking hard. He struck upon an idea!

"Look, Huck!" exclaimed Tom. "On this side of the rock, there are footprints and candle wax but not on any other side. I bet the treasure is buried here."

They began to dig the clay floor at the base of the rock. After some time, when much of the clay was removed, they found a hidden trapdoor!

They quickly removed the wooded planks of the trapdoor and saw, to their amazement, a corridor that began under the rock! They entered and kept walking till they came to a curve in the path.

Tom stopped suddenly and yelled, "Look! The treasure!"

And indeed, they had found the treasure. It was the same big box that they had seen earlier. Tom opened the lid and Huck scooped up gold coins in his clay-covered hands.

"We're rich!" shouted Huck.

The two boys stood there and looked at their treasure for a long time. Then they took out the bags that they had brought with them, filled them with the treasure and slowly, happily, made their way out of the cave.

They looked around to ensure that no one was watching and, after resting for lunch for a few minutes, boarded their bags on the stolen boat and began rowing towards their village. By the time they reached the village riverbank, it was late evening.

They first wondered what to do with the money and then decided to hide it, for the time being, in Widow Douglas' woodshed. They decided to meet the next morning and count and divide their treasure in equal halves.

"You stay here and keep watch," said Tom, "as I go and fetch a wagon to load the bags in. I'll be back in a minute."

So saying, Tom ran towards the village.

He soon came back with a wagon and the two boys loaded the bags of money in it and began dragging it towards Widow Douglas' house.

But before they could reach her house, they had to pass Mr. Welsh's house. He saw them coming up the path and asked, "Is that you, Huck? And Tom?"

He told them to come with him as everyone was waiting for both boys.

Mr. Welsh helped the boys with their wagon, without having a clue as to what it contained. They left it outside Widow Douglas' house. Inside the widow's house, there was a party going on. The Thatchers, the Harpers, Aunt Polly and nearly everyone else from the village were present. Widow Douglas welcomed the two boys, smiling broadly. But Aunt Polly blushed and frowned to see how dirty they both were, covered in dust, clay and candle wax.

Mr. Welsh told the group how he had seen the two boys dragging their wagon on the road outside and had brought them with him to the party.

"You did the right thing," smiled Widow Douglas. "Boys, come with me."

She took Tom and Huck upstairs to a bedroom and gave them each, a set of clothes. There was a shirt, trousers, socks and everything else for each boy.

"We're waiting for you both downstairs. Get dressed and come down and meet us."

So saying, she walked out of the room, leaving the two boys to change.

Chapter Nineteen

A Home For Huck

Huck looked at the new clothes and panicked. He wanted to get out of there.

"I'm not used to this kind of crowd! Let's run away! Is there a rope that we can use to climb down the window?"

Tom laughed and said, "Don't worry, Huck. They're good people. And anyway, I'm here to take care of you."

Then Sid entered the room and said that the party was especially planned for the two boys. Mr. Welsh wanted to announce to everyone how Huck had saved the widow's life. Widow Douglas also had some secret announcement

to make, and she wanted to make it in the presence of Huck.

The boys went to join the rest of the people who were waiting for them. In a dramatic manner, Mr. Welsh told the story of Huck's bravery.

Everyone clapped and the widow hugged Huck and praised him highly. Huck, on the other hand, was feeling very uncomfortable in his new clothes. He didn't like being the centre of attention, either.

Widow Douglas then announced that she would adopt Huck and have him educated. She said that she did not have too much money but had decided to save whatever little she could and start a business for him when he was old enough.

That's when Tom surprised everyone by saying, "Huck doesn't need money. He's rich!"

Rich? The grown-ups all looked at each other. Huck was a poor urchin. How could he be rich?

But without giving any explanation to the questions asked, Tom ran outside to the wagon

where they had hidden their bags of treasure. Every eye was on Huck who could neither move nor speak in embarrassment. Then Tom walked in, bringing heavy bags with him.

He opened the bags and spilled the contents on a table. Hundreds of gold coins covered the table.

"Half of it belongs to Huck," said Tom, smiling as he showed the money, "and other half is mine."

Tom then told everyone about the adventure. They were all amazed. The treasure was counted and it amounted to twelve thousand dollars! Nobody present there had seen such a huge sum of money.

Chapter Twenty

Respectable Huck Joins The Gang

The whole town discussed Tom and Huck's story, adding more details till the real story disappeared underneath the myth. People stared at them wherever they went, and many were envious of their luck. Several men followed their example and began digging up under old abandoned houses to search for treasure. The two boys had become celebrities!

Widow Douglas put Huck's money in a bank, as did Aunt Polly for Tom. Each boy now had an income of a dollar per day!

That week, Becky Thatcher told her father how Tom had taken her punishment on himself in

school one day and was whipped for her mistake. She also told him how Tom had comforted her and given her hope when they were lost in the cave. Mr. Thatcher was very proud of Tom and invited him to their home for dinner. Tom could not have been happier.

But Huck was not happy. He grew up living in dirty, shabby places. Torn, dirty clothes were the most comfortable to him. He could not tolerate the crisp clean clothes that Widow Douglas now made him wear. He hated how her servants kept him clean. Eating at a table with a knife and a fork, and forced to go to church were too much for him.

After three weeks, he ran away. Though search-parties looked everywhere for him, it was Tom who finally found him. Huck had hidden in an abandoned slaughterhouse, wearing his old torn clothes, looking dirty and uncombed but happy.

When Tom urged him to return, Huck said, "I can't do all this anymore! Widow Douglas is very kind to me and I like her. But dressing, cleaning, praying and that too, doing everything at a proper time, is too much for me, Tom. I can't live the way she wants me to."

Huck said "no" to every good reason that Tom gave him to return to the widow's house and live a comfortable life. Then, Tom had a plan.

"Huck," said Tom seriously, "if you don't become respectable, we can't allow you to be part of our gang of robbers. We're forming a gang but you won't be part of it."

"Why?" asked Huck. "I didn't have to be respectable to be a pirate with you."

"But robbers are classy, unlike pirates. Robbers don't have low characters the way pirates do. People will say that Tom Sawyer's gang has low characters and they'll be mean to you, Huck. I won't like it and you won't either."

Huck thought for a long time. He desperately wanted to be part of Tom's gang of robbers. But he had lived on his own, according to his own ways, for so long that he did not want to go back to the disciplined life with Widow Douglas.

"Fine," he said finally. "I'll give it another try for a month more. It's not all that tough, really. But only if you let me be part of your gang."

Tom smiled and the two boys walked together towards the widow's house, talking excitedly about all the adventures that they would have in the days to come.

About The Author

■ Mark Twain

Samuel Langhorne Clemens, better known by his pen name Mark Twain, was an American author, essayist, lecturer and humorist. He wrote a series of famous books including *The Adventures of Huckleberry Finn* and *The Adventures of Tom Sawyer*. He was born on November 30, 1835 in Florida, Missouri in the United States.

Mark's first important work, *The Celebrated Jumping Frog of Calaveras County* was first published in the *New York Saturday Press* and became a bestseller within a short span of time. He also wrote a series of travelogues including the bestselling *The Innocents Abroad* (1869) and notable short stories such as "Advice for Little Girls" and "The Celebrated Jumping Frogs of Calaveras County", which earned him the worldwide fame and appreciation as a writer. Most of all, the author is known for his notable and insightful satires that gained him reverence from both critics as well as his contemporaries who call him the "father of English literature".

■ Characters

Tom Sawyer: The novel's protagonist. Tom was a mischievous and bright boy with an active imagination, who spends most of his time getting himself, and often his friends, into and out of trouble. Despite his mischief, Tom had a good heart and a strong moral conscience.
Aunt Polly: Tom's aunt and guardian. Aunt Polly was a simple, kind-hearted woman who struggled to balance her love for her nephew with her duty to discipline him. She genuinely loved Tom and Sid, and no matter what they did, she never stopped loving them.

Huckleberry Finn: The son of the town drunk and an urchin. Huck is a juvenile outcast who was shunned by respectable society and adored by the local boys, who envied his freedom. He became very close to Tom, as the novel progressed. He also saved the Douglas widow, and in return for his deed she adopted him.

Becky Thatcher: Judge Thatcher's pretty, blonde-haired daughter. She was also Tom's romantic interest.

Joe Harper: Tom's best friend and accomplice. He ran away with Tom and Huck to an island, but was the first succumb to homesickness.

Sid: Tom's half-brother. He enjoyed getting Tom into trouble. He was mean-spirited but presented a superficial show of model behaviour. He thus became the opposite of Tom in the novel, who was warm-hearted but behaved badly.

Injun Joe: A villainous man who committed murder, became a robber, and planned to kill the Widow Douglas.

Muff Potter: A hapless drunk and friend of Injun Joe. He was wrongly accused of murdering Dr. Robinson, but was saved because of Tom's bravery.

The Widow Douglas: A kind-hearted widow, whose husband was a judge. She became a target for Injun Joe to extract his revenge, but was saved by Huck. She later adopts Huck to provide him with a better life.

Judge Thatcher: Becky's father and the county judge.

■ Questions

Chapter 1
- *Why was Tom Sawyer whitewashing the fence?*
- *Who did Tom trick into whitewashing the fence for him and how?*
- *Who did Tom spot by the end of the chapter? What was her name?*

Chapter 2
- *What excuse did Tom make to skip school?*
- *What did Tom do to impress Becky?*

Chapter 3
- *What did Tom give Becky to pacify his mistake? What did Becky do with it?*

Chapter 4
- *Why was Huck carrying a dead cat?*
- *Who did Tom and Huck see in the graveyard?*
- *What did Tom and Huck witness in the graveyard?*
- *What vow did Tom and Huck take by the end of that night?*

Chapter 5
- *Who did the police catch for the murder of Dr. Robinson?*
- *Why did Tom or Huck not open their mouths to defend the innocent?*

Chapter 6
- *What behavioural change made Aunt Polly concerned about Tom?*
- *What did Tom feed the cat?*

Chapter 7
- *Why was Joe Harper sad?*
- *Where did Tom and Joe decide to hide as pirates? Who all were included in the plan?*
- *Explain the adventures the three boys had on the island. Did it last for long and why?*
- *Why was there a steamboat with people in the river?*
- *Who was the first one to suggest about going back home?*

Chapter 8
- *Why did Tom decide to sneak away to the village?*
- *Why did Tom hide in Aunt Polly's room?*
- *Why didn't he leave the note he wrote to Aunt Polly behind, before leaving?*

Chapter 9

- *What plan did Tom have regarding going back home?*
- *Why was everyone present in the church surprised?*
- *Did Tom's plan go smoothly?*
- *Why was Aunt Polly angry at Tom?*

Chapter 10

- *What lie did Tom tell Aunt Polly to pacify her anger?*
- *Why did Tom become a hero for his schoolmates?*
- *What did Tom and Becky do to make each other feel jealous?*
- *Who did Becky see spoiling Tom's spelling book? What did she decide to do about it?*

Chapter 11

- *How did Aunt Polly catch Tom's lie?*
- *How did Tom and Becky mend their differences?*

Chapter 12

- *What did Tom and Huck do to ease their guilt regarding Muff Potter's case?*
- *Which witness managed to give justice to Muff Potter during the trial?*
- *Why did Injun Joe run away?*
- *Why were Tom and Huck scared?*

Chapter 13

- *Why was Tom getting nightmares?*
- *Why did Tom confess during Muff Potter's trial?*
- *Why did Tom and Huck start digging under the trees?*
- *Why did Tom and Huck enter the haunted house on the Cardiff Hill?*
- *Who did Tom and Huck see arguing in the haunted house? What were they arguing about?*

Chapter 14

- *Who were Tom and Huck waiting for near the inn?*
- *Why did Tom ask Huck to run from their hiding spot?*

THE ADVENTURES OF TOM SAWYER

Chapter 15
- *What made Tom forget about Injun Joe and the treasure?*
- *Where did all Tom's friends go for a picnic?*
- *Who was intended target of Injun Joe and the beggar?*
- *How did Huck manage to save the widow?*

Chapter 16
- *How did Tom and Becky get lost in the cave?*
- *Who did Tom see near the cave, which scared him?*

Chapter 17
- *How did Tom and Becky manage to escape from the cave?*
- *Why did Tom faint when he heard that the cave had been sealed off?*

Chapter 18
- *Who was found dead inside the cave?*
- *Where did Tom realise the treasure was hidden?*
- *Why and when did Tom and Huck go in the cave again?*
- *Who were waiting to give a surprise for Tom and Huck?*

Chapter 19
- *Why was Huck nervous to go in front of the people?*
- *Who decided to adopt Huck?*

Chapter 20
- *Was Huck happy with his new life and why?*
- *What did Tom say to Huck to make him stay?*